SHREK THE THIRD

King for a Day, Ogre for Life

Adapted by Judy Katschke

HarperCollins *Children's Books*

The morning sun rose over Far Far Away. Shrek and Fiona woke to the sound of singing birds outside the castle window—and to the annoying sound of a singing Donkey.

"Good morning! Good morning to you."

Shrek sunk under the covers. What was so good about *this* morning? All he had to look forward to was another day as the substitute king!

Puss In Boots marched into the royal bedroom, a clipboard between his paws.

"Okay," he said most efficiently. "You have a very full day filling in for the king and queen."

Shrek was afraid of that. He knew he was just keeping the throne warm while King Harold was sick. But these kingly duties were enough to make him sick, too!

By the end of the day, Fiona, Donkey, and Puss had watched Shrek botch a knighting ceremony and sink one of the Royal Navy's boats instead of christen it. And now they had to get ready for a royal ball.

"Okay, you've had a tough run," Donkey said. "But we are going to make sure you look your best."

Soon Shrek and Fiona found themselves strapped to chairs and getting total makeovers. Shrek cringed as his toenails were trimmed with an electric sander. He winced as his big fat foot was squeezed into a tiny shoe.

Fiona wasn't exactly a pampered princess either. Her nose hairs were painfully plucked. A dainty corset was laced tightly around her big green waist.

"Ow!" Fiona cried.

Once they were finished, Donkey and Puss gasped. Shrek and Fiona looked like two stuffed sausages wearing towering wigs!

Shrek never felt so uncomfortable in his life.

But things were about to get worse. It was time for them to make their big entrance.

"I don't know how much longer I can keep this up, Fiona," Shrek said as they waited to enter the ballroom.

Fiona felt Shrek's pain. Or was it her corset?

"Can you please just try to grin and bear it?" Fiona whispered. "It's just until Dad gets better."

Shrek and Fiona tried to sneak a kiss. But their costumes got in the way. And that wasn't the only problem.

"My butt is itching up a storm, Fiona," Shrek whispered. "And I can't reach it in this monkey suit."

Suddenly, Shrek saw Fiddlesworth carrying a long ruby scepter. A-ha! The perfect itch scratcher!

"Ladies and gentlemen," the master of ceremonies boomed. "Princess Fiona and Sir Shrek!"

The curtain swung open, but Shrek didn't notice. He was too busy getting his itch scratched!

"Um . . . Shrek?" Fiona hissed. "SHREK!!"

Shrek turned to see a shocked crowd. He quickly straightened up, but his belt couldn't hold in his big belly any longer. As his stomach popped out, the belt snapped and the buckle flew across the room—hitting Donkey square in the eye!

"Ow! My eye!" Donkey screamed. He stumbled through the crowd until he fell against a very elegant lady.

"What are you doing?" the lady cried. She gave Donkey a shove. He stumbled against a guard. The guard's ax fell and knocked down a vase. Fiona lunged to catch the vase, only to slip on a puddle of water.

Shrek ran to catch Fiona, but he couldn't keep his pants from falling down. As he tripped, a loose wooden plank flipped Fiddlesworth through the air. Fiddlesworth crashed into a waiter carrying a tray of flaming skewers. The fiery skewers speared into the wall, creating a circle of fire with Donkey in the middle.

"Shrimp!" Donkey said, sneaking a bite. "My favorite!"

Just when the guests thought things couldn't get worse, the smoldering stage began to collapse. Shrek and Fiona watched wide-eyed as the buffet table slid straight toward them.

The entire ball was ruined!

Later, Shrek stormed into the royal bedroom, dripping with appetizers and filled with rage.

"That's it, Fiona!" Shrek shouted. "We're leaving Far Far Away!"

"Honey, please, calm down," Fiona said gently.

Shrek threw aside his wig. "Calm down?" he cried. "Who are we kidding? I'm not cut out for this!"

"Just a couple more days and we'll be back home in our vermin-filled shack," Fiona said softly. "Strewn with fungus, filled with the rotting stench of mud, and maybe the pitter-patter of little ogre feet."

Shrek's green face paled. That meant babies.

"I'm not ready for kids," Shrek said. "Babies just eat and scream and poop—"

"Shrek," Fiona cut in. "Don't you ever think about having a family?"

Shrek wrapped Fiona in his arms. "Right now, you're my family," he said.

There was a quick knock, and the door was flung open. Standing in the doorway was a page.

"Princess Fiona," the page beckoned.

Shrek hated interruptions. "Somebody had better be dying," he growled.

'm dying," the Frog King gasped.

Fiona's eyes filled with tears. She had wished this day would never come.

Queen Lillian, Shrek, Donkey, and Puss stood around the king's lily pad. King Harold had been ill for days. His family and subjects hoped he would recover, but the king knew the truth. He was about to croak.

"Shrek," the king said. "The kingdom needs a new king. You and Fiona are next in line for the throne."

"An ogre as king?" Shrek said. He laughed nervously. "There's got to be somebody else. . . . Anybody?"

"Aside from you there is only one other remaining heir," the king said weakly. "His name . . . is . . . Arthur."

The king hacked. He squeezed his eyes shut before taking one long, raspy breath.

"Harold?" the queen asked.

Fiona cried as she hugged Shrek. Donkey bowed his head, and Puss removed his hat. The king was dead. And Shrek was going to make sure the next king would not be him. He would find this Arthur guy before the crown fell on his own sorry head!

The sun was setting over Far Far Away. A crowd of fairy-tale creatures had gathered on the dock to say good-bye to Shrek, Donkey, and Puss as they set sail to find Arthur.

"I will never forget you," Puss told his pretty kitties. "And you . . . and you . . . and you."

Fiona watched Donkey kiss Dragon and hug his flying, fire-breathing Dronkeys. But she had more than a good-bye kiss for Shrek. She had big news.

"Shrek," Fiona said. "There's something I have to tell you."

"All aboard!" shouted the ship's captain.

Shrek raced up the gangplank to join Donkey and Puss.

"Shrek, wait!" Fiona called.

"What?" Shrek shouted from the boat.

Fiona stood on the edge of the dock and shouted, "YOU'RE GOING TO BE A FATHER!"

Shrek's eyes bugged out. He laughed nervously and opened his mouth . . . but didn't know what to say.

As the boat drifted out to sea, Shrek had to wonder . . . was he ready to be a dad?

3

ot everyone in Far Far Away was wishing Shrek a good voyage. Prince Charming thought nothing but evil thoughts about the ogre as he made his way toward The Poison Apple Inn that night. The prince had great hair and a million-dollar smile, but there was something else he wanted more than anything in the world.

To be king!

Charming entered the stuffy inn. As always, it was packed with fairy-tale villains—like the witches shooting pool and the one-eyed Cyclops riding a bucking mechanical bull. Captain Hook noodled at the piano with his hook-hand, while a snaggletoothed witch belted out a song.

Mabel the ugly stepsister stood behind the counter polishing glasses with her spit.

"What do you want, Charming?" Mabel demanded.

"Refreshments for all of my friends!" Charming declared in a loud voice.

Everyone stopped what they were doing to glare at Charming. Captain Hook knocked over the piano bench as he stood up. "We're not your friends," he growled.

Charming gulped as the pirate dug his needle-sharp hook into his throat. He knew it was a tough crowd—but not this tough!

"Wait!" Charming blurted. "We are more alike than you think!"

Charming turned his eyes to the bitter Evil Queen. "The seven dwarfs saved Snow White and left you the un-fairest of them all," he said. "How does that feel?"

"Pretty unfair," the Evil Queen admitted.

"Frumpypigskin." Charming turned to Rumplestiltskin. "Where's that first-born baby you were promised?"

The evil dwarf grumbled under his breath.

"And Hook," Charming said. He cast his eyes downward at the gleaming hook. "Need I say more?"

Hook frowned as he lowered his hook-hand. Charming knew he was on a roll now!

"Once upon a time someone decided we were the losers!" Charming shouted. "But our side of the story has never been told!"

The villains mumbled in agreement.

"Who will join me?" Charming demanded. "Who wants their happily-ever-after?"

The villains cheered, then celebrated with a knockdown, drag-out brawl. Charming smiled as he ducked to avoid a flying chair. The time had come to take the throne. And this time no one would get in his way!

hrek's boat had reached its final destination. But all Shrek could think about was his scary dream from the night before: hundreds of drooling, pooping ogre babies calling him Daddy.

Shrek knew he wouldn't make a good dad. Just like he knew he wouldn't make a good king. His gloomy thoughts were interrupted by the voice of Donkey:

"Wor-kess-ter-shurry. Now, that sounds fancy!"

Shrek, Donkey, and Puss stood at the entrance to the castle. A sign read WORCESTER-SHIRE ACADEMY.

"It's Worst-uh-shur," Shrek corrected.

"Like the sauce?" Donkey cried. "Mmmm!"

The drawbridge to the castle was lowered.

As Shrek, Donkey, and Puss marched in, a horse-drawn school bus rolled by. Kids screamed out of the windows when they saw Shrek.

"My stomach aches and my palms are sweaty," Shrek gulped. "So it must be a high school!"

"High school?" Donkey cried. "I'm starting to feel sick from memories of wedgies!"

Puss didn't get it. "How did you receive the wedgies when you are clearly not the wearer of the underpants?" he asked.

Donkey didn't answer. Some things were better left unsaid!

Shrek, Donkey, and Puss walked along the school grounds.

Perky cheerleaders were practicing a new cheer. Shiny horse-drawn carriages were lined up in the school parking lot. Two pimply kids sat hunched over a board game.

"Where can I find Arthur?" Shrek asked.

One kid pointed to two knights on horseback. All Shrek noticed was the brawny knight in the gleaming armor.

That's got to be Arthur! Shrek thought.

The knights began to joust. Hooves thundered on the ground as their horses charged toward each other. The brawny one aimed his lance—and sent his geeky opponent flying off his horse and through the air!

"Does Arthur look like a king or what?" Shrek asked with a smile.

The geek looked up from the ground. "Just so that you know," he said, "Arthur goes by his nickname, Peaches."

Shrek stared at the supersized knight. Did he say . . . Peaches?

The handsome steed reared its hooves at the sight of the big, green ogre. The attractive student tumbled off onto the ground.

"Greetings, Your Majesty," Shrek said. "This is your lucky day."

Shrek tossed the knight over his shoulder. "We're late for your coronation, Peaches," he said.

"Peaches?!" the knight shouted. "What are you talking about? My name is Lancelot!"

Shrek froze. If this guy was Lancelot, then Arthur must be . . .

He turned to see the geek slipping into the school building. In a flash, Shrek, Donkey, and Puss were inside the school, trolling the halls looking for the real Arthur.

"Oh, Arthur!" Shrek called. "Come out, come out, wherever you are!"

Inside the gymnasium, kids lined the bleachers. Principal Pynchley smiled as he shouted into a megaphone:

"And now, without further ado, let's give a Worcestershire huzzah to the winner of the New Mascot contest!"

Standing next to the principal were two mascot contestants: a student dressed as a unicorn and one wearing a griffin costume. Both crossed their fingers inside their fuzzy mitts.

"And the winner is the—"

The doors burst open and in walked Shrek.

"Ogre?" Pynchley squeaked.

Students cheered. The marching band played. Shrek grabbed the principal's megaphone and shouted, "Now, where's Arthur?"

No answer.

"Come on out, Arthur!" Shrek shouted. "I know you're in here!"

"Hey, monster!" Lancelot yelled. He pointed behind Shrek. Hanging from the basketball hoop with the mother of all wedgies was Arthur!

"Would you mind coming down?" Shrek asked. "You're the new king of Far Far Away."

"Artie a king?" Lancelot guffawed. "More like the Mayor of Loserville!"

Big laughs filled the gym.

Puss used his sword to cut Artie free.

"All right, kid," Shrek said, catching Artie. "Let's go get you fitted for your crown."

Artie finally got that it wasn't a joke. It was the moment he had been waiting for all his life!

"Woo-hoo!" Artie cheered. He turned to the crowd in the bleachers. "Enjoy your stay here in prison while I rule the free world!"

Everyone watched in amazement as Artie strutted out through the doors with Shrek, Puss, and Donkey. The king of all wedgies was about to be *king*!

ack in the castle in Far Far Away, Fiona sat perfectly still as bluebirds lowered a garland of flowers onto her head. It wasn't exactly her style, but it was her baby shower and she was going to go along with whatever was planned.

"It's present time," Snow White declared.

"Open mine first, Fiona," Cinderella said.

Fiona read Cinderella's card out loud: "Congratulations on your new mess maker. Hopefully this helps."

Fiona pulled a small shovel and a plastic bag from the gift box.

"It's for the poopies!" Cinderella laughed.

"Oh!" Fiona politely laughed, too.

The Three Little Pigs and Wolf stepped forward.

"We all chipped in for a little present, too," one Pig said.

"Ta-daaa!" Pinocchio sang. He spread his wooden arms to reveal a baby carrier slung over his chest. Nestled inside was a very cozy Gingerbread Man.

"You know the baby is going to love it," Gingy said. "Because I do."

"That's so sweet," Fiona said. "Thank you."

While the party continued inside the castle, Prince Charming was outside, hatching a sinister plan.

"Onward, my new friends!" Charming shouted. "To our happily-ever-after!"

Charming and the fairy-tale villains zoomed toward downtown Far Far Away on witches' broomsticks.

"Now, bombs away!" Charming ordered.

Using evil trees as parachutes, the villains touched down on the busy street. Captain Hook and the Headless Horseman galloped in on horseback.

Screaming villagers fled as the villains trashed everything in sight. But for Charming it was just the beginning.

"To the castle!" he declared.

At the same time, Fiona was opening Snow White's present. Out of the box hopped a dwarf.

"He's a live-in babysitter!" Snow White explained.

"What does he do?" Fiona asked.

The princesses answered at once: "The cleaning! The feeding! The burping!"

"What are Shrek and I supposed to do?" Fiona asked.

"Don't expect Shrek to be helpful," Rapunzel said. "He'll be out with his buddies all night."

Fiona's eyes widened.

Shrek wouldn't do that . . . would he?

"How did Shrek react when you told him?" Doris the ugly stepsister asked.

Fiona remembered the special moment on the dock when she told Shrek the big news. She also remembered the stunned look on his green face as the boat pulled away.

"Um, Shrek?" Fiona said. "He was . . . uh . . . very—"

She was interrupted by a loud ROAR!

Everyone ran to the window and looked out. Witches were dropping a heavy net over Dragon. The castle was under attack!

"Everybody stay calm," Snow White said. "We're all going to die!"

But the fairy-tale creatures took action. Pinocchio and the Three Little Pigs piled furniture in front of the library door.

"You go and take care of the baby," Gingy told Fiona. "We'll hold them off as long as we can."

Fiona raced to the fireplace and pushed it aside. Behind it was a secret tunnel.

"Everyone in! Now!" Fiona ordered.

The queen and the princesses slipped through the tunnel just as the villains broke down the door. Charming looked around for Shrek and Fiona. All he found were fairy-tale creatures having a tea party.

"Where are Shrek and Fiona?" Charming demanded.

"Names don't ring a bell," Gingy said.

"Yah!" a Pig agreed.

Captain Hook raised his hook over Gingy. When the pastry wouldn't crumble, Charming turned to Pinocchio.

"You can't tell a lie," Charming snapped. "Tell me, where is Shrek?"

"Well," Pinocchio said. "I don't know where he's not."

Charming narrowed his eyes at Pinocchio. "You're telling me you don't know where Shrek is?" he growled.

Pinocchio tried hard not to lie. "I do or do not know where he shouldn't probably be!" he said.

"So you *do* know where he is!" Charming said.

"Even if he wasn't *not* where I knew he was could mean that I wouldn't completely not know where he wasn't." Pinocchio panted.

Charming gritted his teeth. He was getting nowhere. Until one of the Pigs squealed.

"Shrek went off to bring back the next heir—oh!" He clapped his hammy hoof over his mouth. But it was too late.

A sly smile spread across Charming's face.

"Hook," he ordered, "get rid of this new king. But bring Shrek back to me!"

hanks for getting me out of there, Shrek. That place was a dead end," Artie said later on the boat back to Far Far Away. "But this is gonna be huge! Parties! Princesses! Castles!"

Artie couldn't believe his good luck. "Am I really the only heir?" he asked.

"The one and only," Shrek lied.

"Sweet!" Artie declared. So far, so good.

"You'll have the finest chefs," Donkey said, licking his chops.

"And royal food tasters!" Puss added. "They taste the food to make sure it's not poisoned."

"Poisoned?" Artie gasped.

"You will bask in the affection of your subjects," Puss said.

"Just make sure they don't die of famine or plague," added Donkey.

"Plague?" Artie squeaked. He couldn't believe his ears. Being king made Worcestershire Academy seem like a fun park!

"Come on now." Shrek chuckled. "We don't want Artie to get the wrong idea."

But Artie already had an idea—to turn the ship back. In a flash, he was at the wheel, spinning it around.

"Artie!" Shrek grabbed the wheel and spun it the other way. "What are you doing?"

The boat veered right and then left as Shrek and Artie fought over the wheel. A seasick Donkey tried hard not to barf!

"What does it look like?" Artie said, turning the wheel toward his school. "I don't know anything about being king! I'm going back!" Artie glared at Shrek. Why hadn't he told him being king would be such a drag?

"Back to what? Being a loser?" Shrek asked, then instantly regretted it.

Shrek's words hit Artie like a ton of bricks. He let go of the wheel, leaving Shrek to pull on it hard—so hard that the steering wheel came off in his hands!

Now there was nowhere for the boat to go but straight ahead toward shallow water and jagged rocks.

"Land ho!" the captain shouted as the boat crashed.

The shaken passengers disembarked. Shrek turned to Artie and snapped, "This isn't getting you out of anything. We're going to Far Far Away and you're going to be a father!"

Everyone stared at Shrek.

"I mean . . . king! You're gonna be king!"

"Yeah, right," Artie muttered. He turned and marched up a path that led to the woods.

"You get back here, young man, and I mean it!" shouted Shrek.

Puss looked up at the ogre. "Uh, boss? I don't think he's coming back."

The three friends trudged up the path after Artie.

Up ahead, Artie saw a cottage and got an idea. When he saw Shrek coming up behind him, Artie took off toward the cottage, shouting, "Somebody, help! I've been kidnapped by a monster!"

"Calm down, kid!" Shrek called.

Artie pounded on the door. A burst of light shot out. Donkey and Puss clutched each other as the image of an old wizard's face appeared to float in the air. What was going on?

"Attention, trespassers!" the face boomed. "Vacate the premises pronto or prepare to suffer the wrath of—"

FZZZZZ-BLOOP! The face disappeared. Out from the cottage walked a tiny old man.

"Mr. Merlin?" Artie asked.

"You know this guy?" Shrek asked.

"He was the school's magic teacher," Artie explained.

Merlin invited the travelers to stay for dinner. Donkey thought he meant the stew cooking on the fire, so he stuck his snout in and started to guzzle . . . but it was a cauldron full of underpants!

"Get away from my laundry!" shouted Merlin.

"Thanks, but we've got a lot of ground to cover," said Shrek. He grabbed Artie's arm so they could leave.

"Why don't you go terrorize a village and leave me alone?" snarled Artie.

A fed-up Shrek gritted his teeth. This new king was turning out to be a royal pain!

"Understand this, kid," Shrek growled. "It's no more Mr. Nice Guy from here on out."

Merlin was fed up with all the arguing, too. It was time for his guests to do a little wizardly soul-searching!

"You're not going to get anywhere unless you learn to confront your inner demons," explained the wizard.

He grabbed a handful of dirt and tossed it into the campfire. Plumes of smoke billowed in the air.

"Look into the smoke," Merlin directed, "and tell me what you see."

Donkey saw something yummy.

Puss saw someone pretty.

Shrek saw a stroller with a baby in it, but he lied to the group.

"I see a rainbow pony," Shrek said.

Artie narrowed his eyes at Shrek.

"Now the boy," Merlin said.

"I see a guy, and he's standing in front of a castle," Artie said slowly. "Whoa! The castle's got teeth and it's chasing him!" He gasped. "It ate him!"

As the smoke cleared, Shrek, Donkey, and Puss stared at Artie.

"Whoa, you're really messed up," said Merlin. Then he turned to go into his cottage. "Nighty-night!" he called.

Artie plopped down on a log and looked glum.

Donkey and Puss signaled Shrek with their eyes to go talk to Artie. They looked at Artie and then looked at Shrek. Then looked at Artie again and then at Shrek again. Shrek heaved a big sigh and sat next to Artie.

"I know you want me to be king," said Artie, "but I can't. I'm not cut out for it and I never will be. Even my own dad knew I wasn't worth the trouble. He dumped me at that school, and I never heard from him again."

"My dad was an ogre," Shrek said sympathetically. "He tried to eat me!"

For the first time, Artie cracked a smile.

"People used to think of me as a villain," Shrek explained. "But just because people call you a terrible monster, it doesn't mean that's what you are."

Artie thoughtfully poked the embers with a twig. Maybe the ol' Shrekker wasn't such an ogre after all.

"You know, you're okay, Shrek," Artie said. "You just need to do a little less yelling. And use a little more soap."

"Thanks, Artie," Shrek said with a smirk.

Merlin's dinner guests sat quietly around the fire. The flames were still crackling. But the smoke had definitely cleared.

iona's torch lit their path as the party of princesses made their way through the dark tunnels under the Far Far Away castle.

"Where are we going?" Cinderella asked.

"Stay close," Fiona said. "There's another entrance to the castle around here somewhere."

Sleeping Beauty yawned as Doris carried her through the tunnel. "We've been walking for hours," she said. "My feet are killing me."

"This place is filthy," Cinderella complained.

"I'm sorry," Snow White complained. "But this just isn't working for me."

"Everything is always about you, isn't it?" Sleeping Beauty argued.

Fiona tried hard to ignore the bickering. She took a few more steps until she finally found what she was looking for. A ladder!

"That's it!" Fiona said.

Climbing a ladder in a princess gown wasn't easy. But soon the escapees were crawling out through a grate into the castle courtyard.

Fiona and the princesses peeked around a corner. An outdoor theater was being built.

"This way," Rapunzel said. She began running toward the castle.

"Rapunzel, wait!" Fiona called. She and the others raced after Rapunzel. When they burst into the castle, they saw Prince Charming holding her by the arm!

"Charming, let go of her!" Fiona ordered.

"Why would I want to do that?" Charming asked, flashing his pearly white teeth. Then Charming and Rapunzel exchanged a kiss.

"Say hello to the new queen of Far Far Away!" Charming said.

"Rapunzel, how could you?" Fiona cried.

"Jealous much?" Rapunzel asked, flipping her hair.

"Soon you'll be back where you started," Charming told the princesses. "Scrubbing floors or locked away in towers."

"Shrek will be back soon, and you'll be sorry!" Fiona said.

"On the contrary," Charming said, "I'm counting on his return. The play wouldn't be complete without Shrek's big finish."

Royal guards dragged the queen and princesses off to prison. Fiona knew they had to save Shrek. But first they would have to save *themselves*!

Shrek woke with a start. He, Donkey, Puss, and Artie had dozed off around the campfire. It was now morning, and the sun was streaming through thick forest leaves.

Donkey was still snoring like a buzz saw, Puss was taking a serious catnap, and Artie was fast asleep on a log.

Just then a dark shadow fell over Shrek. He turned, and his eyes popped wide open. A bunch of evil trees were lumbering straight toward them.

The trees raised their twisty branches as they surrounded the campsite. The log under Artie sat up, knocking him to the ground.

"Good morning," an evil tree said as he loomed over Donkey.

"Good morning." Donkey yawned. He blinked open his eyes. But when he saw his wicked wake-up call, he yelped.

Shrek saw Captain Hook between the trees. The villain grinned as he played a lively tune on his piano.

"King Charming has something special in mind for you, ogre," Hook sneered.

King Charming? Before Shrek could ask about Fiona, the captain shouted, "Attack!"

A gang of pirates swung forward on tree branches. Instead of hands—or hooks—they had forks, knives, and whisks. The utensils became weapons as the pirates attacked Shrek and his friends.

"Arrgh! Arrgh!" the pirates growled.

Puss fought the villains. But his sword was no match for the dozens of swinging spoons and spatulas.

Hook kept playing his piano as the pirates forced Shrek to walk a plank. Shrek fell off the edge into an open treasure chest. The swashbucklers cheered as the lid slammed shut.

Meanwhile, evil trees scooped Puss, Donkey, and Artie up in a net. Donkey gnawed and Puss clawed the net as the pirates aimed a loaded cannon at them. Just when they thought they were goners, Shrek burst out of the chest.

"Help!" Artie shouted.

Shrek thought fast to save his friends. He tossed the treasure chest onto the other side of the plank. The plank seesawed, flipping Shrek over to the cannon. Quickly, he turned the cannon in the other direction and blasted Hook's piano to smithereens!

The villains knew they were defeated. The evil trees dropped the netting that held Donkey, Puss, and Artie. Then the trees and pirates took off running, leaving Hook behind!

"Cowards!" Hook shouted after them.

"What has Charming done with Fiona?" Shrek demanded.

"She's gonna get what's coming to her," Captain Hook said. He raised his hook in the air, only to get it caught in a twisted tree branch.

"Ahhhh!" Hook screamed as the runaway tree dragged him away. "And there's nothing you can do to stop Charming."

"Mr. Merlin!" Artie shouted, as they raced into his camp. "We need a spell to get us back to Far Far Away!"

"Forget it," Merlin said. "I don't have it in me anymore, kid."

Artie begged and begged. When that didn't work, he sobbed and sobbed.

"Okay, okay." Merlin sighed. "I'll go and get my things."

Artie winked at Shrek. Merlin had fallen for his little performance!

Merlin came back with a spell book. "I'm a little rusty, so there may be side effects," he said. "But they'll wear off sooner or later . . . I think."

Everyone listened as Merlin began to chant: "Alacraticious expeditions, a zoomy-zoom-zoom. Let's help four friends get back . . . um . . . soon."

Magic rays zapped from Merlin's fingertips. Shrek, Donkey, Puss, and Artie disappeared in a flash.

Merlin blew on the tips of his fingers and looked around. The spell had worked!

A few seconds later, Shrek, Donkey, Puss, and Artie plunged from the sky. They landed in a heap on a street in Far Far Away.

"Oh, man," Donkey said. "I haven't been on a trip like that since college."

"Donkey?" Shrek said.

"What's wrong?" Donkey asked. He looked down and shrieked. Instead of a donkey tail, he had a fluffy cat tail! And instead of donkey fur, he was wearing boots!

"At least you don't look like some bloated roadside piñata!" Puss said from Donkey's body.

Shrek and Artie couldn't believe it. Merlin's spell had zapped Donkey into Puss's body and Puss into Donkey's.

But Donkey and Puss weren't the only things that had changed. As they walked through Far Far Away, they couldn't believe their eyes. Graffiti covered the walls. Carriages lay in the street with broken wheels. Almost every store window was smashed!

"It wasn't like this when we left," Shrek told Artie.

He turned at the sound of jingly music. A wooden boy on strings was dancing inside a coin-operated puppet theater.

"Pinocchio?" Shrek said.

"Shrek, help me!" Pinocchio cried through the glass.

The ogre put in some coins, and the curtain opened.

"What happened?" Shrek asked.

"Charming and the villains took over everything!" Pinocchio said quickly.

"Where is Fiona?" Shrek cried.

"Charming's got her locked away somewhere secret," Pinocchio said. "He's probably getting ready for the show!"

The curtain fell, and Shrek was out of coins.

"What show?" Shrek cried.

Pinocchio's hand slid out from under the curtain. It pointed to a poster on the wall. It showed Charming slaying a green ogre.

"It's the ogre!" a voice shouted from behind. "Get him!"

Royal knights surrounded Shrek and his friends. As they pointed their sharp weapons, Artie thought fast. He stepped out in front.

"Look," Artie said to the guards. "Don't you know who he is? How dare you!"

Shrek got it. He started acting like a spoiled movie star so he could get safely into the palace.

"I don't know who dropped the ball on this," Shrek said to the guards, "but the carriage was supposed to pick me up at my hotel."

"He's a star, people!" Artie demanded, pointing at

the poster. "You can't treat a star like this!"

Their little act worked. Before they knew it, Shrek, Donkey, Puss, and Artie were being personally escorted to the castle.

Meanwhile, Charming entered his dressing room. He plopped into the chair at his dressing table and adjusted the mirror. He saw his handsome face—and Shrek, Donkey, Puss, and Artie standing in the doorway.

"Break a leg," Shrek growled. "On second thought, let me break it for you."

"Thank goodness you're here," Charming said with a sly smile. "I was afraid you might not make it back in time."

"Where's Fiona?" Shrek demanded.

Guards burst into the room. Sneaky Charming had pushed a secret alarm button under the table.

"Let me guess," Charming said, studying Artie. "You're Arthur?"

"It's Artie," Artie replied.

"This boy is supposed to be the new king of Far Far Away?" Charming laughed. "How pathetic."

Shrek didn't want Artie to get hurt. He had to protect him. And the only way to do it was to come clean.

"That's enough, Charming," Shrek said. "This isn't about him."

"Then who's it about?" Artie asked in confusion. "I'm supposed to be king, right?"

"You weren't really next in line for the throne," Shrek said. "I was."

Artie's jaw dropped. Shrek knew he was breaking the boy's heart. But a broken heart was better than broken arms or legs!

"I said whatever I had to say!" Shrek yelled. "I wasn't right for the job, and I needed some fool to replace me. Just go!" Shrek felt terrible saying these things, but he *had* to get Artie away from Charming.

"You've been playing me the whole time!" Artie cried. "I actually thought you—"

"Cared about you?" Charming cut in. "He's an ogre. What did you expect?"

Shrek caught Artie's hurt expression as the guards led him out of the dressing room.

"You really do have a way with children, Shrek," said Charming with a sneer.

Maybe I am just a selfish ogre, Shrek thought sadly. *Boy, am I going to be a lousy father.*

9

Fiona gazed through the bars of the prison window. Where was Shrek? And exactly what was Charming planning?

"Had we just stayed put," Snow White grumbled, "we could be sipping tea out of little heart-shaped cups."

Doris tried to pry apart the prison bars. But they were steelier than she was.

"Who cares who's running the kingdom anyway?" Snow White grumbled.

"I care!" Fiona answered.

"And you all should, too," the queen said.

Just then the huge iron door flew open. Donkey and Puss were hurled into the cell.

"Donkey? Puss?" Fiona cried.

"I am Puss, Princessa," Puss said from

Donkey's mouth. "Stuck here inside this hideous body!"

"And I'm me," Donkey said from the body of Puss.

"Where's Shrek?" Fiona asked.

"Charming's got him, Princess," Donkey said. "He plans on killing Shrek tonight in front of the whole kingdom."

Fiona was *not* going to let that happen. "All right, everyone," she said. "We need to find a way out, now!"

"Ladies," Snow White declared. "Assume the position."

Sleeping Beauty fell asleep. Snow White puckered her lips. Cinderella dusted a spot on the floor and sat down.

"What are you doing?" Fiona asked.

"Waiting to be rescued," Snow White said.

"You've got to be kidding!" Fiona cried.

The queen pushed her way through the damsels in distress.

"Excuse me," she said. "Old lady coming through."

She stopped in front of a brick wall. *"IIiiiiiii-yyyyiiiiaaah!"*

Everyone gasped as the queen head-butted a hole through the brick wall.

"Mom?" Fiona said.

"You didn't think you got your fighting skills from your father, did you?" the queen asked.

Fiona smiled. Leave it to a queen to use her head!

"Okay, girls," Fiona said. "Do you want your happily-ever-after back or not?"

Those were the magic words. Fighting words!

Snow White ripped off her sleeve to show her dwarf tattoo. Sleeping Beauty ripped off the bottom of her dress. Cinderella sharpened the heel of her glass slipper.

The princesses placed their hands over Fiona's. So did Donkey and Puss. The fairest in the land—and the furriest—were ready to rumble!

One by one the prisoners escaped from the cell. Then they quietly made their way toward the castle.

As they peeked out from behind a log they saw the evil trees guarding the gate to the castle. Fiona signaled Snow White. As she began to sing, gentle forest creatures gathered around her. But when Snow's song turned into a battle cry, the animals turned on the trees and attacked.

"Move it!" Fiona shouted. "Go! Go! Go!"

Stampeding princesses took on charging guards. Cinderella threw her glass slipper like a boomerang, knocking a guard out cold. Sleeping Beauty fell asleep on the ground, tripping more charging guards. Doris didn't have a glass slipper, but her fist punched through the lock, and the gate flew open.

With enough guards taken out, the queen and princesses climbed the wall to the castle roof.

From there Fiona could see the theater. The stage was set for Charming's sinister show.

Meanwhile, Puss and Donkey had rounded up their fairy-tale friends, and another type of show was about to be staged—a showdown! They too would storm the castle and save Shrek!

"Let's do this thing, people!" Donkey shouted as he marched in Puss's boots. "Go Team Dy-no-mite!"

"Um, Donkey, sir," Pinocchio said. "I thought we agreed to go by the name Team Supercool."

"As I recall it was Team Awesome," Gingy stated.

"I voted for Team Alpha Wolf Squadron!" Wolf complained.

"All right, all right, all right!" Donkey groaned. "From now on we'll be known as Team Alpha Super Awesome Cool Dynomite Wolf Squadron!"

Just then an angry Artie stomped by. The fairy-tale creatures tried to stop him, but he kept on walking.

"You knew what was going on, and you kept it to yourselves," Artie snapped.

"Artie, it's not like it seems," Donkey said.

"Oh, really?" Artie mumbled. "It seemed like a setup from the start! He never believed in me."

"Didn't Shrek teach you anything?" asked Donkey. "Don't believe everything everyone says about you!"

"Shrek only said those things to protect you!" Puss added.

Artie stopped walking. He thought about what Donkey and Puss had said. Suddenly, it made sense.

Shrek had helped him. Now it was his turn to help Shrek!

s Shrek waited backstage, he wanted to bring down the house—with his bare hands. But his heavy chains kept him from moving an inch.

"Ladies and gentlemen!" the announcer boomed. "The Far Far Away Theater is proud to present 'It's a Happily-Ever-After, After All.'"

A spotlight hit the stage. Charming rose from beneath the stage on horseback.

"I'm strong and brave," Charming sang. He flipped his hair and grinned. *"And dashing..."*

Costumed villains joined Charming in a rousing song-and-dance number. Backstage, Mabel roared through a megaphone. Three witches turned a lever. A hush fell over the audience as the shackled Shrek rose through a trapdoor in the stage.

"Please rescue meeeee," Rapunzel sung from a stage-set tower. *"From this monstrosity!"*

Charming whipped out his sword. He pointed it at Shrek's chest and sang, *"You are about to enter a world of pain with which you are not familiaaaaaar!"*

The high note shattered glass tiaras, goblets, and eyeglasses—and Shrek's eardrums!

"It can't be any more painful than your lousy performance," Shrek scoffed.

Everyone laughed, except Charming. He cleared his throat and tried again. *"Prepare, foul beast . . . ,"* he sang.

"Have mercy!" Shrek groaned. "Kill me first!"

More laughs.

"Enough!!" Charming screamed.

The audience fell silent.

"Now you'll finally know what it's like to have everything that's precious to you taken away!" Charming snapped.

He raised his sword in the air. He was about to bring it down on Shrek

when—ZAP! A fireball melted the blade, courtesy of Dragon and the Dronkeys flying above the stage!

Charming froze as more fairy-tale creatures stormed the stage. Even the queen and princesses burst their way through the scenic backdrop.

"Hi, honey," Fiona said, hugging Shrek. "Sorry we're late."

Charming wasn't about to give up. With a clap of his hands he summoned the villains. The terrified audience watched as good clashed with evil right there on the stage. But this time it wasn't a show—it was the real deal!

Shrek tried to free himself from his shackles, but it was no use. Charming seized the moment—and another sword. He was about to raise it when a powerful spotlight shone in his face.

"Hold it!" a voice shouted.

"What is it now?" Charming groaned.

Shrek smiled as he looked up. Jumping from the spotlight was Artie. He swung from a fake cloud, landing between the villains and Shrek.

"Wait!" Artie said. "Who really thinks we need to settle things this way?"

All villain hands shot up.

"You're telling me you just want to be villains your whole lives?" Artie went on. "Don't you ever wish you could be someone else?"

Charming commanded the villains to attack. But Artie had their full attention.

"It's hard to come by honest work," an evil tree explained, "when the whole world's against you."

"A good friend of mine once told me that just

because people treat you like a villain, it doesn't mean you are one," Artie said. "The thing that matters is what you think of yourself."

Shrek smiled as he recognized his own words.

"What is it you really want?" Artie asked the villains.

"I always wanted to learn the guitar!" the Headless Horseman shouted.

"I'd like to open a spa in France!" the Evil Queen said.

"I grow daffodils!" Captain Hook declared. "And they're beautiful!"

Villains and fairy-tale creatures threw down their weapons and shook hands. But Prince Charming wasn't ready to give up his dream—he wasn't going to let anyone stand in his way to the throne! Grabbing a sword, he charged Shrek!

"Ahhhhhhh!" Charming shouted.

Shrek tried to step aside, but the chains got in the way. Fiona gasped as Charming's sword rammed straight into Shrek's belly.

"Shrek!" Fiona cried.

But Shrek just smiled. He lifted his arm to show that the sword had gone between his arm and his side without hurting him. He grabbed Charming and lifted him off his feet.

"This was supposed to be *my* happily-ever-after!" huffed Charming.

"Well, I guess you need to keep looking," said Shrek as he looked at Fiona, "because I'm not giving up mine."

Shrek set him down and nodded to Dragon. She flicked her tail at Rapunzel's tower, toppling it over like a house of cards.

"Momm-eeeeeee!" Charming cried.

The tower came down on Charming with a crash. His crown popped off and rolled across the stage. Shrek picked it up and held it out to Artie.

"It's yours if you want it," Shrek said. "You've got what it takes, kid."

Artie took the crown. He turned to the audience. Then Arthur Pendragon lifted the crown and put it on his head!

The crowd went wild. Fairy-tale villains and fairy-tale creatures lifted the new king on their shoulders and began to cheer.

"Ar-tie! Ar-tie! Ar-tie!"

In a puff of smoke, Merlin suddenly appeared, clutching his ticket to the show. Donkey and Puss immediately pounced on him.

"The time has come to rectify some wrongs!" declared Puss.

"Because I'm not doing any more of these 'cat baths,'" Donkey said from Puss's body.

"All right, all right!" Merlin said, rubbing his hands together. "You're gonna feel a little pinch, and

possibly some lower intestinal discomfort, but this should do the trick."

The wizard rolled up his sleeves. With a burst of magic, he zapped Donkey and Puss back to their own bodies.

"I'm me again!" Donkey exclaimed.

"And I am not you!" Puss said with relief. They walked away together, laughing. After they turned, Merlin could see that Donkey still had Puss's fluffy tail and Puss still had Donkey's gray tail.

"Oops!" Merlin said. Then he shrugged and walked away.

Despite the shambles of Charming's stage show around them, Shrek and Fiona were having a happy ending.

"I think you would have made a great king," Fiona said.

"No," Shrek said. "I have something much more important in mind."

And when burping, wailing, and pooping babies soon filled their swamp shack, Fiona understood.

Shrek didn't need to be a great king because he was a great dad!